COOL CATS MAKE HATS

BOOK 9

by Hara Lewis
Illustrated by Matt Straub

SCHOLASTIC INC. Cartwheel B·O·O·K·S ®

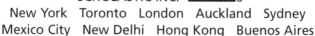
New York   Toronto   London   Auckland   Sydney
Mexico City   New Delhi   Hong Kong   Buenos Aires

Cool cats like hats.

Each cool cat
will make a hat.

Pam makes a beach hat.

Tom makes a peach hat.

Matt wants a noisy hat.

He makes one that beeps.

Pat makes three hats.

One hat is a frog hat.

One hat has a bee.

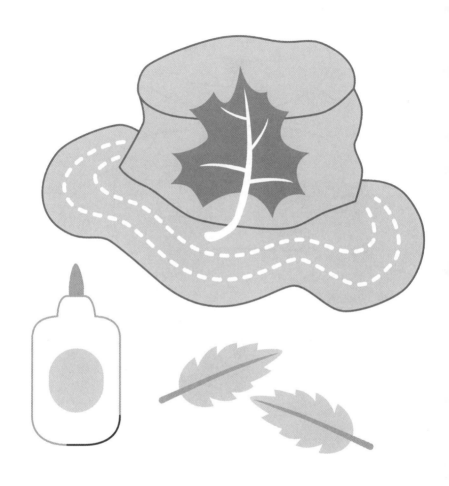

One hat has a leaf.

"I want one more cool hat,"
says Pat.

What hat can she make?

"Make a hat with a beak,"
says Tom.

Pat makes a hat with
a beak.

"See my hat," says Pat.
It is cool, indeed!